Dossier 001:
THE POSTMAN ALWAYS BRINGS MICE

A Novel by **Holm & Hamel**

Illustrated by Brad Weinman

HarperCollinsPublishers

Library of Congress Cataloging-in-Publication Data

Holm & Hamel.

The postman always brings mice / by Holm & Hamel ; illustrated by Brad Weinman.—1st ed.

p.   cm. — (The stink files, dossier 001)

Summary: A dashing British feline spy is dismayed to find himself stranded in New Jersey and adopted by a typical suburban family, until he puts his skills to good use for his new human.

ISBN 0-06-052979-2 — ISBN 0-06-052980-6 (lib. bdg.)

[1. Cats—Fiction. 2. Spies—Fiction. 3. Mystery and detective stories.] I. Weinman, Brad, ill. II. Title. III. Series.

PZ7.H732226Po 2004   2003017550

[Fic]—dc22   CIP

                                                                            AC

Typography by Karin Paprocki

1 2 3 4 5 6 7 8 9 10

❖

First Edition

To a certain princess with beautiful black fur.
You were always the best at sniffing out mice.
—James

Dossier Contents

I WAS RUNNING in the rain.

Not a soft, misty London rain that feels like flannel on the fur, but something more akin to a hurricane. Thunder split the sky and lightning struck within mere inches of me. This was the kind of torrential storm only America could produce.

It was raining—if you'll pardon the expression—cats and dogs.

A driver leaned on his horn as his car flashed past, and I was drenched by a tidal wave of muddy water. I ducked left as a motorcycle rumbled past, skidding to avoid me.

Six lanes to cross. Then five. Then four.

Blinking stinging water from my eyes, I dodged blindly, narrowly avoiding a massive black truck. The car behind it locked its brakes and swerved left. I went right.

Three lanes left. Two. I leaped.

And lost my footing, yowling as I slipped in a puddle and nearly decorated the grille of a minivan. I scrambled to my waterlogged paws and spun around to see—

A pair of headlights bearing down on me!

My life flashed before my eyes. One down and eight to go.

I could hardly believe that I, James Edward Bristlefur, who had dined with royalty, who had foiled devious conspiracies thicker than cream, who had brought the long paw of the law down on international criminals— that I, in short, was going to die in America.

In a town that does not even have an opera, I might add.

1

Security Is Compromised by Shortbread

IT WAS on account of a biscuit that I came to find myself in the middle of the road in the pouring rain. But let me go back to the beginning.

My human, Sir Archibald, was the Director of MI9, Britain's most secret counterspy agency. His was a shadowy group, far behind the scenes, vastly more secret than MI5, 6, 7, or 8. So secret, in fact, that "MI9" is not even the organization's real name. A vow of absolute silence, to which Sir Archibald was required to swear each year, prevents me from revealing even that. What I can tell you, however, is that the organization we shall call MI9 maintains a constant vigil against spies, thieves, assassins, and other generally bad guys.

On the day that changed my life forever, the British Security Service (the comparatively un-secret MI5) intercepted intelligence that a group of master spies was planning to kidnap the Queen during the Masked New Year's Eve Ball at Buckingham Palace.

Sir Archibald was informed immediately. He mobilized all available personnel to establish a secure perimeter. Meanwhile, he himself would serve personally as a last line of defense, blending in among the Queen's guests with two of his best agents at his side. The trio departed for the palace dressed, appropriately enough, as the Three Musketeers.

Sir Archibald and I were very close, and most days I could be found prowling around MI9 headquarters, a kind of office mascot. A spy's life is a lonely one, and quite often Sir Archibald would bring me along for company in the field as well. But that night, he left me behind in his quarters, a very nice townhouse on a quiet Westminster mews, only a few blocks away from the palace.

"Stay here tonight, cat, and keep an eye on things," Sir Archibald said on his way out the door. He winked. "After all, we don't have a costume for you."

And with a flourish of his musketeer's cape, he was gone.

Now, I am a cat of breeding, and honor demanded that I stay put. Not all cats are honorable, to be sure, but educated cats are schooled to value the Feline Code of Honor above all else.

As the evening wore on, however, I grew more and more agitated. Something was not right.

Sir Archibald had always valued my instincts, and I had never disappointed him. For example, when I jumped on his pillow to wake him in the middle of the night, he knew I was not begging to be let out like a common cat: experience had taught him to be instantly alert, listening for any intruders I had detected. Those same instincts were now telling me that Sir Archibald needed me. I slipped through an open window and into the chill evening air.

The streets of southwest London were nearly deserted, with everyone indoors preparing for the stroke of midnight. In moments, I found myself standing in front of Buckingham Palace.

Having been with Sir Archibald since kittenhood, I had acquired many useful skills, such as the ability to silently infiltrate a gathering of humans. When I slipped through the bars of the palace gates, the four sentries posted there—tall humans in fancy red tunics and ridiculous bearskin hats—did not even glance in my direction.

Obtaining access to the ballroom itself was a simple matter, as I had long ago developed a good rapport with the palace rats. Don't be surprised: even a palace has rats. Rodents of all kinds are easy to intimidate and make valuable informants, and the palace rats were familiar with the back ways and secret passages.

I circulated silently among the costumed guests, looking for suspicious behavior. Nothing seemed to be amiss until I spotted the sleek Siamese and knew mischief was a-paw.

She was curled innocently by the roaring fireplace on a leopard-skin rug. As I drew closer, she yawned and looked at me drowsily through half-lidded eyes of startling blue. Siamese cats are as beautiful as they are intelligent, and their facility with language makes them very popular as companions for master spies.

I followed the lady as she stretched and then headed toward the pastry tables. Even if she was innocent, she was quite captivating and certainly worth a closer look, I reasoned. A most delicious perfume wafted from her well-groomed fur.

When I reached the pastry table, I paused to lick a

small dollop of whipped cream that had fallen to the floor, and I lost her in the press of human legs and feet. I sank low to the ground and peered into the corners just in time to see a slender, black-tipped tail disappear through a door leading to a darkened side chamber. I prowled closer to investigate.

The chamber was temporarily serving as the ballroom's coat closet and was full of elegant overcoats and hats and intriguing-smelling furs. I slipped inside and sniffed the air.

A voice behind me drawled, "And vat's your name, handsome?"

She may have been a Siamese, but the accent was Russian. That tipped me off immediately. But danger and perfumed cats are an intoxicating combination, so I played along. She was half my size, I told myself. I could handle her with both paws stuck to a tree.

I spun around. She was leaning lightly against the door frame, haloed from behind by the ballroom lights.

"The name is Bristlefur. James Edward Bristlefur." I bowed gallantly. "Are you with one of our guests?"

"How very puuurceptive."

She nosed closer, her breath smelling enticingly of salmon. I closed my eyes and felt her whiskers brush against mine.

"Oh, James," she murmured. "It's a pity you have to go, just as things are getting so interesting."

"Go?" I said. "Where am I going?"

And with that, the door to the coatroom smacked me in the nose, and I found myself alone, locked in darkness.

It was not the first time a lady had complicated my life.

Leaping quickly to a low table by the door, I put one eye to the antique keyhole just in time to see the minx saunter into the crowd of humans, twitching

her tail back and forth proudly.

It was then that I spotted the two waiters carrying large trays of tasty-looking canapés. *Salmon* canapés. The same flavor I had smelled on the lady's breath. I moved closer, the fur on my back rising.

Peeping out from beneath the waiters' aprons were Uzi compact submachine guns—a favorite among enemy spies!

I had no time to lose.

Extending a long, well-sharpened claw between the door and the doorjamb, I flicked the bolt and pushed hard with my head—a trick I had picked up from watching Sir Archibald in action. The blackguards with the machine guns were inconspicuously working their way around the refreshments toward Her Royal Highness, who was deep in conversation with the boring Prince of Draakenstein.

My low-pitched yowl of warning instantly alerted Sir Archibald and his agents, who drew their swords and tackled the villains as they tried to hide behind a pudding. The Siamese, however, had vanished without a trace.

Needless to say, I had saved the day. Or rather, the evening.

Hours later, after the champagne had been drunk

and the guests had gone, Sir Archibald and I retired to his townhouse to enjoy a well-deserved saucer of cream for me and a cup of tea and some of his favorite Scottish biscuits for him.

"Job well done, cat," Sir Archibald said with a tired smile.

Then my first human companion, my dear Sir Archibald, took one bite of a shortbread biscuit, gripped his throat, and pitched over onto the floor.

Dead.

2

What Happens to Lost Luggage

Now you must understand, our tale has just
begun, but I had known Sir Archibald from
kittenhood.

I had been raised on the farm of an exclusive cat
breeder in the south of France, surrounded by other
cats of exceptional promise. Although my mien and
markings were unmistakably those of a Bengal, the
noblest of cats, I had been found in the woods nearby,
a blind newborn, and no one knew my true parentage
for certain. I had worked particularly hard to compen-
sate for this, but even so I never quite fit in with the
other kittens.

One day, a British spy named Archibald Ash visited the farm, pulling up the long gravel driveway in his bright-red Jaguar C-Type. I knew from the moment I saw the man—and the car—that we were made for each other. Fortunately, he felt the same way, and I was packed off to England.

Training for my first assignment lasted well over a year, for it transpired that Archibald had scouted the entire continent for the perfect cat to provide his cover story for a mission. He was on assignment to track a nefarious international arms dealer known for his stockpile of stolen nukes—and for his hobby of breeding showcats. (And let me note here that although we eventually captured the man and his prize-winning cat collection, his favorite—a six-toed white Persian named Macavity—somehow vanished from his yacht off the coast of Monte Carlo.) The operation exceeded all expectations for success, earning Archibald his knighthood and me an enduring place by his side.

In the years that followed, as Sir Archibald rose quickly through the ranks of MI9, we spent many happy hours together. He took me anywhere a well-behaved, well-bred cat would not be unwelcome—attending formal events, listening in on espionage training sessions, or sitting by his side during tedious all-night stakeouts. Summer evenings would often find us driving through the streets of London or Paris in his open Jag, the wind ruffling my fur as I sat in the passenger seat. In short, I knew Sir Archibald better than any man or cat on Earth, and I was crushed when he died.

In the days following the tragic event, I could not get off the bed in his old townhouse, not even to eat. For you see, I blamed myself. Someone had infiltrated our home while I was out, and the biscuits had been poisoned.

I stared at the biscuit tin, with its cheery painting of a Norwegian fjord, still sitting on Sir Archibald's favorite table in the tea nook at the window. The tin was now empty (the contents having been sent for lab analysis) and was covered with black residue from fingerprint dust. I stared and stared until my eyes could no longer focus, as if by staring I could see through time and space to find Sir Archibald's killer. At last, delirious from grief and hunger (and cross-eyed from staring), I allowed myself to be bundled into a traveling cage by Miss Astrid, Sir Archibald's lovely young secretary.

Sir Archibald had been a bachelor, and a spy has few friends: there was really no other place for me to go. In the days that followed, Miss Astrid nursed me back to health in her small flat near Regent's Park, occasionally dragging me, blinking, into the park for fresh air and exercise.

"The lab rats in Scotland Yard say no fingerprints were found in the townhouse, Master Bristlefur," one of my informants, a local field mouse, told me during one of these outings. "They was professionals, all right."

One evening at home as Miss Astrid was sadly sorting through a box of things from Sir Archibald's office, she gave a loud sneeze. She had been doing a lot of this lately—sneezing, that is. She looked at me, her eyes watering, her nose red.

"Listen, cat"—and here she sneezed again—"I know you can't understand me, but I want you to know that you've made it a lot easier for me to cope with losing Sir Archibald."

If only humans knew just how much we do understand.

"You're such a dear, but— *achoo.*" Sneezes always come in threes. "But I'm allergic to you, and I just can't keep you any longer. My sister-in-law in Norway wrote me that she'd love to have a big, beautiful cat like you. I think a little country air would do you good, don't you?"

Norway! Suddenly an image flashed into my head: the biscuits Sir Archibald had eaten that night had *not* been his usual Scottish favorite! The tin I had stared at for so long had been marked "Product of Norway." Someone had switched the biscuits! *Only I, who knew Sir Archibald so well, could possibly have noticed this detail.* And by perfect coincidence, I was being sent to Norway! I would spend a few days at Miss Astrid's sister-in-law's, getting my bearings, and then I would strike out on my own and bring Sir Archibald's killer to justice.

That night, I slept well for the first time in weeks, dreaming dark dreams of revenge. In the morning, Miss Astrid bundled me into a carrier, and we drove off to Heathrow Airport. My last image of Miss Astrid was of her peering sadly at me, wiping her red eyes, as a cargo handler snapped a baggage tag onto the cage. I looked around just in time to see the needle looming large.

And then everything went dark.

The next thing I knew, I heard a distinctly American voice drawl, "I think this one's dead."

I opened my eyes a squint, and the world swam in and out of focus.

Dimly, I remembered banging around in the carrier for a long, long time and hearing two cats talking in hushed voices. One had a thick Norwegian accent, and the other spoke in low, ominous tones. Vaguely familiar ominous tones.

With a few blinks, my vision grew clearer. I was still in the carrier, only now enormous piles of luggage surrounded me in a cavernous room.

Perhaps I *was* dead—although this was hardly my idea of cat heaven.

"You dead, cat?" the deep voice asked, and someone gave me a firm poke.

I bit the finger hard, testing my fangs. The man promptly let out a roar.

It seemed I was not dead after all.

However, I soon wished I were. For you see, instead of arriving in Norway, I had somehow been misdirected to Newark Airport.

In New Jersey.

In the United States of America.

3

Imprisoned without Trial

I **WAS TAKEN** to the Humane Society.

Even now, I shudder when I recall my long, horrible weeks of confinement. What had possessed them to call this place humane? First I was tortured: pinned to a stainless-steel table and subjected to innumerable pokes, prods, needles, and tests. Then I was shoved into a tiny paper-lined cage.

I nearly lost my breakfast when a tremendous stench hit my nostrils, but as my stomach was empty, all I could do was retch. More than half the cage was taken up by an enormous lump of mottled, grayish fur that seemed to be the source of the horrible smell. And then as I watched, it opened a pair of eyes! Or not it, *he*. The pile of fur was actually an enormous, overweight, long-haired cat of uncertain pedigree. He must have weighed close to forty pounds.

My cell mate and I stared at each other for what seemed a long time.

Finally, I remembered my manners and extended a paw. "The name is Bristlefur, James Edward Bristlefur," I said.

"Bugsy," he said, scratching at a patch of matted fur he could barely reach because of his bulk. "But everybody calls me Bugs."

On second thought, I withdrew my paw.

Our cell block contained row upon row of cramped steel cages stacked to the ceiling, full of wretched animals meowing, growling, and hissing at the humans who occasionally walked through. Most cages were shared by two cats, but a good many contained three, and the kittens were crammed together by the dozen.

And I, a well-bred cat of unquestionable taste, packed among them like a peasant.

I may not have known my parentage, but I knew I was a Bengal. Of all the small cats, we Bengal are most closely related to the great barbarian kings of the African plains. The legend is even told among kittens that somewhere in the mountains is a secret kingdom

of cats—Catlandia—where the Bengal rule undisputed over all other breeds. Of course this is just a fairy tale, but a well-educated Bengal like myself is traditionally accorded the respect of nobility.

My cell mate, however, did not care one bit about my royal connections. Nor did he care to let me sleep in the nicer part of the cage, closer to the door, where the air was freshest. And so I was obliged to sleep at the back, right up against the cage of Ralph, a pathetic street cat who meowed every five seconds without surcease.

Ruffian.

By the end of my fifth week in captivity, I had fallen into a mindless routine, shuffling from my cage to the exercise yard and back each day. I was growing gaunt and malnourished, and my fur was beginning to fall out from lack of sleep. Worse, every moment I spent stuck in this place allowed Sir Archibald's killer more time to cover his tracks.

"Why the long face, Jimmy?" Bugs asked me one day. "It ain't so bad in here." Seeing my skeptical look, he added, "Hey, you should see some of the families I been with."

One of Bugs's more annoying habits, apart from his

personal hygiene, was his refusal to use my proper given name, alternately calling me "Jim," "Jimmy," and "Jimbo."

"Ahh, don't worry, Jimbo. You'll get adopted one of these days. And if you don't like 'em, just lie down by the side of the road and pretend you been hit by a car. I do it all the time."

Nevertheless, try as I might, none of the visiting humans seemed to notice either of us. Perhaps they were driven away by the smell. Finally, late one afternoon, an adult female human came in accompanied by a slender, freckled boy with curly brown hair and an even smaller girl, who was holding a doll and picking her nose.

"Can't we go look at the dogs?" the boy was saying to the larger human, presumably his mother. "I don't want a cat. I want a dog! Cats are stupid."

I blinked. He didn't look like a rocket scientist himself.

"Then we can go home right now," his mother retorted. "I've told you a thousand times, no dogs!"

"Look at the kitty!" the little girl giggled, ignoring the others and pointing—with the index finger that was not presently up her nose—directly at me.

I could have kissed her.

"I don't want a stupid cat," the boy repeated, ignoring his sister. "I want a dog!"

"Too bad. You're not responsible enough for a dog."

"I am so!"

"Are you going to feed him every day?" she continued. "Walk him three times a day so he doesn't poop in the house? Take really good care of him?"

"Yes!"

"Like that gerbil of yours?" There was a trace of sarcasm in the mother's voice.

"That wasn't my fault! Lily let him out of the cage!"

"I did not!" said the little girl, paying attention now.

"Did so!"

"Did not, did not, did not!"

"Will you two *settle down*! Maybe I should just leave you both here and get *two* cats," the mother said, exasperated.

Remarkably, the children stopped bickering.

"Okay, okay, we'll take the cat. Jeez, Mom," the boy said, wandering over to my cage.

The mother sighed. "Look, maybe when you're older we can talk about getting you a dog. Think of this as a step up from gerbils."

The boy was peering in at me. "Well, I guess this one's okay for a cat," he conceded doubtfully. "He is kind of big and tough-looking."

I regarded him through slitted eyes. Of course I was tough. Furthermore, I was also an experienced covert operative. I stretched and flexed my claws.

The little girl backed away.

"He's too big. And he's scary-looking," she whined. "I want a little baby fluffy cat. With long white fur I can brush." She stroked her doll's yarn hair with what were evidently sticky fingers.

"It's up to your brother," the mother said. "It's going to be his cat, so he gets to decide."

The boy stared at me, and I stared right back defiantly.

"Well," the boy said reluctantly, "he's better than nothing."

I was stuffed into a cardboard cat carrier, and that was that.

4

Out of the Cage and into the Dungeon

I **COULD NOT** see much through the airholes of the cardboard cat carrier, but one thing was clear. I was in a grape-colored minivan.

A minivan!

To think that a few short months earlier, I had been riding around London, enjoying the musky leather fragrance of the front passenger seat of Sir Archibald's brand-new Jaguar XKR convertible. The backseat of the minivan, on the other hand, smelled of barf.

Oh, the indignity of it all.

The XKR's magnificent, supercharged 4.2-liter V8 engine could send delicious purring rumbles through your body, especially if you curled up on the floor of the front seat during a long drive. From the sound of the minivan's pathetic V4, we would be lucky to get wherever we were going in one piece. The alternator's timing was noticeably off, and there was little doubt that the oil filter was well past needing a change.

I was something of an expert on cars. Sir Archibald had owned a small collection of Jaguars, from the brand-new XKR to the classic 1953 C-Type I had first seen him drive. On lazy Sunday afternoons, he used to let me lie on top of a warm car while he worked on the engine. I knew the purr of a healthy, high-performance machine when I heard it, and Sir Archibald had learned to watch the flicking of my tail for signs that there were problems beyond the range of mere human hearing.

Awash in memories of Sir Archibald, I peered miserably out the holes of my cardboard box at the passing scenery just as a large, green road sign flashed by. "Welcome to Woodland Park, New Jersey," the sign boldly proclaimed.

Woodland Park. That didn't sound so bad. And the license plate on the minivan had proclaimed this the Garden State.

Perhaps everything I had heard about America was untrue.

★ ★ ★

We pulled directly into a dank garage smelling intensely of old cut grass and spilled petrol, so I did not have a chance to view the surrounding neighborhood. Reconnaissance would have to wait until later.

"Why don't you put him in the laundry room while I go fix him up a litter box?" the mother said.

"Can't I keep him in my room?" the boy asked.

"No, he stays in the laundry room," his mother replied. And then, seeing his expression, she added, "Maybe in a few days. We'll see. I don't want him ruining the furniture."

As if.

Sir Archibald had owned an exquisite collection of antique furniture—genuine Hepplewhite sideboards, Persian rugs, Victorian velvet settees. And I had never laid a claw on anything.

Nevertheless, if I was to be locked in some laundry room, I had merely exchanged one form of captivity for another. I had to find a way to gain control of the situation and escape. "A few days" was too long to wait to get my mission back on track.

The boy carried me into an unfinished basement and set the cardboard carrier down on the lid of a washing machine. As soon as he opened the flaps, I stepped out, turned around, and sat up neatly to examine him. The boy was clearly unnerved by my behavior, precisely my intention.

Sir Archibald used to tell his human operatives that in a hostage situation it is important to try to establish a personal relationship with one's captors—to encourage them to view one as an individual.

Upon closer inspection, the boy appeared quite unextraordinary: a little on the spindly side but with a certain intelligence about the eyes. With persistence, I ought to be able to manipulate him. Growing increasingly unnerved by my scrutiny, the boy muttered, "Stupid cat," and left me alone.

Unfortunately, everyone left me alone. I found myself in the basement laundry room with a shoe box filled with strips of torn-up newspaper. As if I were a rabbit. Or a gerbil. Or just demented like Auntie Bella, an old matriarch at the cat farm who was afraid of mice.

My new accommodations were even worse than those at the Humane Society, if that was possible. The laundry room was dark and damp and smelled of detergent and stale socks. It had a painted concrete floor, one slim window high on the wall, and two doors. One door, through which we had entered the house, led directly to the garage. From what I could glimpse when the family locked me in the room, the other led into a carpeted, wood-paneled, basement rec room and, presumably, to the rest of the house. I tested both doors and found them firmly closed. Neither door had any nearby furniture to jump onto, so I could not use my lockpicking skills.

As I looked around the room, the gravity of my situation started to sink in. Here I was, a prisoner in a strange house an ocean away from where I was supposed to be, and the trail of Sir Archibald's killer was growing colder by the moment. I felt, suddenly, quite overwhelmed and exhausted.

Without even bothering to lick the stench of the Humane Society, not to mention Bugs, from my fur, I curled up atop the warm dryer as it *thump-thump*ed, tumbling the family's socks and pants and towels. I closed my eyes and drifted off, my thoughts full of the comforting sights and sounds of London.

Of napping on the smooth bonnet of a classic Jaguar warming under the sun.

Zzzzzzzzzz.

A bright flash, like lightning, woke me.

I blinked away spots to discover the mother and her

two children crowded around the clothes dryer, peering at me. The mother was holding a camera, poised to take another picture.

"Doesn't he look precious?" she was saying.

I could feel something stuck to the top of my head. I shook vigorously, and that something fell to the floor. It was an adhesive Christmas bow. A pink one.

"Let's call him Mr. Pink," Lily said, giggling.

I shook my head vigorously, and the bow came loose and fell to the floor.

"No way," the boy said. "He's not a girl, Lily. He's a very tough tomcat who eats little girls for breakfast."

How unappetizing.

"I know that! That's why I said *Mr.* Pink. Duh!"

"Mr. *Stink* is more like it," the mother chimed in wryly. "Phew! Maybe we should give this cat a bath."

A bath? Over my dead body!

5

Contact with the Underground

REALLY DID smell awful.

I had already bathed myself twice from head to toe and was halfway through a third cleaning when I heard a familiar scurrying. I leaped to the concrete floor as quietly as I could and padded silently in the direction of the furnace, to the shadowed depths of the basement, where the sounds seemed to be coming from.

As I inched closer, I could make out two distinct voices echoing in the small space between the back of the furnace and the wall.

"Tree kernels a' dried corn? For a moldy hot dog?

You tryin' to cheat da fur off my back? Yer outta yer mind, Frankie!" squeaked a high-pitched voice with a heavy American accent.

"A deal's a deal, Vinnie. Don't you *rat* on me."

Both mice snickered, completely oblivious to what was about to happen to them.

I struck like lightning, scattering the small pile of stolen food they had been arguing over. My paw neatly pinned the smaller of the two rodents.

"AAAAH! Don't eat me!" the little one shrieked, squirming as his companion backed into a corner, his mouth working wordlessly.

"Eat you?" I said, aghast. "Whyever would I do that?"

In proper London society, mice understand the unspoken law of the chase—that they were created for the amusement of cats. Certainly, there are occasional accidents in which mice are injured, but only the most low-class mousers and poachers catch mice for any purpose but sport.

"Because dat's what you cats always do. Eats mice!"

"Well, I can assure you I have no intention of eating you. Rather unsportsmanlike, don't you agree? One might play with a mouse for a while, but consume: never."

The mice cast hopeful glances at each other.

"So you ain't gonna eat us, for real?" asked the other mouse.

"All I require from you," I said impatiently, "is instructions on how to get to Newark Airport." Stowing away on a flight to Norway would be more difficult, I thought, but I would cross that fence when I came to it.

The two mice looked at each other in confusion.

"Nyooerk? Nevah hoid of it," the little one said.

"Shut up, stupid," the other one said, smacking the first. "Dat's his weirdo accent. You know Newark, da car service on Twelfth."

They began arguing. "Who you calling stupid, stupid? Dat's New *Yawk* Car Service, and it's on Thoid," the first mouse retorted.

"What do you know? You never been there, Frankie!"

"Neitha have you, Vinnie!"

I interrupted them impatiently. "Don't you two know anything about the geography around here?" *Americans*, I thought.

"We ain't never been farther than da end of da block," the little one whined.

"Yeah, dat's Bruno's territory."

"Bruno, you say? And who exactly is this *Bruno*?

Can he, perhaps, direct me to the airport?"

The two mice exchanged a sly glance.

"Sure . . . Bruno knows everything. He's got family all over New Jersey."

"Yeah, why don't you go an' see him? Tell 'im we said 'how you doin'?'"

And with that they burst out laughing. The smaller mouse seemed to have forgotten that he was still under my paw. I pricked him lightly with a claw, and he immediately sobered.

"Just go to da end of da block. You won't need to find 'im, he'll find you," the mouse said, looking frightened again.

I nodded and raised my paw, and the two of them scampered frantically into the darkness without so much as a by-your-leave, leaving their ill-gotten goods in the dust behind the furnace.

Clearly these two mice had been raised in the gutter.

Judging by the light, it was late afternoon. I was feeling a bit drowsy and was tempted to take another nap, but after the affair of the pink bow, I didn't want to risk letting my guard down. Also, I was starting to wonder when my jailers had scheduled mealtimes—if they kept me locked up in here much longer, perhaps

I would consider eating the mice after all.

Just then, I heard the garage door open with a thundering rumble, and a moment later a second car pulled inside, its engine booming in the enclosed space. A 1972 MGB, from the sound of it, although it should have been obvious to anyone that the sports car needed a new carburetor and higher-octane petrol.

In a few moments, an adult male human, presumably the children's father, entered through the door to the garage, carrying a plastic bin and a large shopping bag marked "Parkside Pet Supplies."

"So how are you settling in, cat?" the man said to me. He was a stocky fellow with graying sideburns and light-brown curly hair much like his son's. His full beard was also curly. Overall, he reminded me of the Russian embassy accountant Sir Archibald had once bribed as an inside contact.

"I hear they're calling you Mr. Stink. I don't smell anything." He chuckled.

I glared at him and barely resisted the urge to roll my eyes.

Something large and heavy clattered down the stairs like a herd of stampeding deer, and a moment later the boy came through from the rec room.

"Hey, Dad," the boy said. "Did you bring home the stuff from the store?"

"Yep," replied the older human, holding up the bag. "Best thing about owning a pet food store, we get to try out all the new stuff. Gotta test it before we can sell it, right?"

What did they think I was? A lab rat?

"This is a new kind from Mexico." The father pulled out a large sack of dry food that said *Arriba Arriba! For a Peppy Cat!* "Whadd-ya say? Wanna give Mr. Stink his first meal?"

"Okay," the boy said. "But don't call him Mr. Stink. That was Mom's idea. I haven't officially picked a name for him yet."

The hard, dry pellets made a pinging sound as his father filled a metal bowl for me. Most unappetizing. My sensitive ears were picking up something else, however: the whistle of air through a tiny gap in the connecting door to the garage. The door was slightly ajar!

"He's a beautiful cat, Aaron. You did a good job picking him. Here." The father handed the bowl of food to the boy.

"A dog would have been better," the child grumbled.

The father was still admiring me. "So well behaved

too. I bet he could be a showcat. Most cats would be screaming their heads off for you to put the bowl down by now." Most pathetic cats with no sense of decorum, I wanted to say. The father nudged the boy to put the food down. "Go on and give it to him."

The boy stooped and put the metal bowl on the floor, eyeing me without enthusiasm.

When he straightened, I leaped down from the clothes dryer and made a show of sniffing at the food—actually, it didn't smell that bad—rubbing against their legs in mock affection as a diversion. I tensed my back legs . . .

. . . and bounded toward the connecting door, thrusting one paw beneath the door and wrenching it open!

"Hey! Get back here, you . . . Mr. Stink!" they both shouted after me.

I slipped through, slunk under the minivan, and made for the driveway.

6

Deceived by a Lady

MY HEART sank when I got a better look at this so-called Woodland Park.

I had expected the surroundings to bear at least some resemblance to Regent's Park in London, with its tree-lined walks and hundred-year-old roses. But from what I could tell, Woodland Park had no woodlands. And certainly no parks. A few square yards of brown grass appeared to be the only vegetation of any kind. In fact, Woodland Park resembled nothing so much as an endless stretch of cracked pavement, crowded on either side with dreary houses and slush-filled gutters.

Realizing that the mice had not clarified which end

of the block was Bruno's, I chose a direction at random and wandered along the sidewalk, eyes darting around for pursuers. When the house was fully out of sight, I sat on the curb and tried to keep warm while I pondered what to do next. In espionage, it is vital not to run off half-groomed without a plan, especially in an unfamiliar situation with inadequate intelligence.

Then I noticed the footprints in the muddy snow.

I deduced from the depth of the impressions that they had been left by a large dog—perhaps one hundred pounds. He appeared to walk with a slight limp in his right hind leg, which might indicate early signs of hip arthritis, a condition common to German shepherds and shepherd mixes. I didn't need to smell him to know he would be trouble.

Could this be Bruno? The mice had certainly encouraged me to assume that Bruno was another mouse, but I had seen right through their deception.

Mice are never as clever as they think they are.

I followed the prints as they wound down the block. But I heard Bruno's name before I saw him.

"No, Bruno, no!" a voice shouted.

Unless I was very much mistaken, that was a lady's voice. A lady cat's voice! I looked up and saw that all my conclusions were correct. Bruno was . . .

a gigantic . . .

nasty . . .

ugly . . .

brown-and-black . . .

Rottweiler–German Shepherd mutt!

In other words, precisely the dog I had been expecting.

At the moment, he was growling throatily at an adorable, if rather skinny, gray cat trapped in one of the sickly, leafless saplings that passed for trees in Woodland Park. Bits of dog drool spewed in all directions as Bruno barked like a shotgun.

A thoroughly distasteful creature. And dangerous.

Bruno leaped up and pressed his paws against the slender trunk, shaking the branches. The young lady yowled in terror as she whipped back and forth through the air.

Did I mention she was adorable? Perhaps the reader has noticed that I have a bit of an eye for the ladies, even though it has often gotten me into trouble.

"Help me!" she mewled.

I sprang to her defense, drawing the dog's attention with a hiss and a loud growl, puffing my fur up to its full extent. Many a dog or cat—or even human—has

lost its nerve and fled in terror when confronted with an angry Bengal.

But not Bruno. Merely taken aback, he settled to the ground and looked at me quizzically.

"Well, don't just stand there," the young lady called down when she noticed me. "Do something! Scratch 'im!"

Despite her alluring classic looks, her accent revealed her to be American. And, I'm afraid, quite common.

Nevertheless, I pressed forward with honor. "Unpaw her, you ruffian!"

"This ain't none of your business," the dog snarled, recovering from his surprise.

"I am making it my business."

"Yer makin' a mistake, is what yer makin', cat."

"The mistake will be yours, if you do not leave off this instant," I countered.

I slashed at the air in front of him with one paw. I took pride in the proper care and cleaning of my claws, and they were long, curved, and extremely lethal.

The dog paused uncertainly.

"Quickly," I urged the lady.

She scampered down the tree, but when she reached the bottom, she stumbled, and something spilled out of her mouth. She had been carrying a small pile of dry, round bits in her cheeks like a squirrel. I leaned forward, sniffing.

Dog food?

"Hey," she said, moving forward quickly to snatch up the food again.

I eyed Bruno more carefully. Behind him was the saddest-looking doghouse I'd ever seen. There was a gaping hole in the roof. In front of the house was a bowl of fetid rainwater, and next to that an unsanitary plastic dog food bowl. An empty bowl, I might add. And while Bruno was clearly a full-grown male, several of his ribs were showing, and his haunches looked quite thin. Either his neglectful family did not feed him, or . . .

"That cat's been stealing my food for weeks now!" Bruno said.

But the young lady just laughed over her shoulder and beat a hasty retreat. Bruno swung his baleful gaze on me.

"I believe I may have misjudged the situation," I said tentatively.

"You can say that again," Bruno growled, advancing on me.

Suddenly, I felt a hand seize me by the scruff of the neck, and I was lifted bodily into the air.

During the confrontation, I hadn't even noticed the

sound of the car pulling to a stop behind me. But sure enough, the dreaded minivan was parked beside the curb.

"There you are, Mr. Stink," the boy's mother said as she put me into the cardboard cat carrier on the passenger seat. "Bad cat. You had us worried."

"Mr. Stink, eh?" A wide smirk spread across Bruno's muzzle.

As the car door closed and we drove away, I heard him threaten, "I know where you live, Stink!"

7

A Model Prisoner

I **WAS TOSSED** back into my laundry room dungeon to a chorus of the mother and father repeating "Bad Cat" as if I were an imbecile.

Sir Archibald always told his agents they should never stop gathering information, especially when captured. As in many houses, this basement had a network of rectangular metal ducts hanging a foot beneath the ceiling. I knew these ducts were vented throughout the house, so they would be perfect for eavesdropping. In fact, for someone with my keen hearing, they were as good as a well-placed bug.

I leaped to the dusty top of the nearest one, wincing as my feet landed on the thin metal and raised a loud roll of thunder. Squeezing myself into the small space between the duct and the ceiling, I pressed my ear against the duct.

"Did you hear that?" This from the mother.

"Maybe that cat knocked something over." The father.

"Want me to go check?" This was the boy's voice. I tensed.

The mother sighed. "No, what's done is done. We can look after dinner. Finish your carrots, Lily."

The father spoke up. "So, kiddo, you want to do anything special for the sleepover this weekend?"

At this, the boy mumbled something too indistinct for me to hear.

"What was that?"

"I said I'm not having a sleepover. Robby and Paul can't make it."

"Neither of them?"

"No, okay? Just forget about it," the boy said in a tight voice.

There was silence upstairs for a few moments.

"I have an idea," the mother said. "Why don't you have a cat sleepover? You can take him up to your room tonight, if you want."

I pictured his sullen shrug clearly in my mind's eye.

"May I be excused?" the boy said.

The little girl piped up. "Can I have the cat tomorrow night?"

"We'll see. Go ahead, Aaron."

I heard the boy's footsteps cross over my head as the little girl continued.

"You always say 'we'll see'! Why can't we get two cats? I don't like Mr. Stink!"

"Lily, for the last time, finish your carrots."

"Thb—there!" Lily gargled around a mouthful of food.

"Okay, you can go too." As the girl took off at a run, her mother called after her, "And no spitting them out in the bathroom."

The clink of utensils on plates told me the parents ate silently for a minute or two. I idly peered across the room from my perch and sniffed . . . fresh air? And it was coming from the very back of the basement! Near where I had seen the mice earlier. I was about to investigate when I heard the mother say in a quiet voice:

"I'm worried about Aaron. He's having a really tough time at school."

"That's what it's like when you move to a new neighborhood. He'll make friends."

"He has. That's what I don't understand. It's like

they all dropped him for some reason. Will you talk to him, please? He won't talk to me about it."

"All right. Why don't you bring him the cat, though? Might cheer him up."

The moment I heard her chair scrape against the floor upstairs, I was off the duct like a shot, darting for the dryer. I was safely atop it when I heard the door open at the top of the basement stairs.

Then I saw them.

I had left little black pawprints all over the painted floor and the white enamel dryer.

The mother started down the stairs.

The less these humans knew about my movements, the better. It was the one advantage I had over them.

I leaped down from the dryer and slid across the floor like a rugby forward diving across the try line, smearing the dust up into my fur and erasing the pawprints.

The mother was at the bottom of the stairs now, heading across the rec room carpet to the laundry room door.

I raced back and wiped away the marks on the dryer.

The door opened slowly.

She found me sitting there innocently, licking my fur back into place. For good measure, I blinked up at her blearily, as if I had just awakened from a nap. She eyed the untouched food bowl.

"You sure are a finicky cat, Mr. Stink. That's supposed to be premium stuff." She pretended to smell the food with relish. "Mmmm. I love Mexican food."

You eat it then, I thought. She wasn't fooling anyone.

She moved to pick me up. "C'mon. Let's go see the rest of the house."

I avoided her grasp. Getting out of the dungeon would be most welcome, but I was not about to be carried like a lapdog. She reached again, and again I dodged out of the way, looking at her defiantly the whole time.

"Okay, so you don't want to be carried." She frowned down at me. "Don't you want to come upstairs?"

Some humans are none too bright, particularly Americans, or so I had been told by more than one French cat I had known. I jumped down to stand beside her, an indication that I would be a cooperative prisoner and follow wherever she led me.

She gave me an appraising look. "Howard's right; you must have been a showcat."

I looked back at her steadily, lifting one paw and flicking my tail in impatience.

Really, it is so difficult to train humans sometimes.

★ ★ ★

The mother led me up the wooden stairs, past a kitchen and a sitting room, down a hallway, and up another flight of stairs. She kept glancing back at me to be sure I was still following. I considered it wise to do as she expected, lest I find myself locked up in the basement again. Or worse, carried.

We proceeded down a long, carpeted hallway to a doorway with a sticker proclaiming, "Only Astronauts Allowed In."

"Aaron?" she called, knocking softly.

There was no answer.

She knocked again, then opened the door gently. "Aaron, I have, uh, Mr. Stink here."

The room smelled of peanut butter. Inside, the boy was glued to a small television set, playing some sort of video game. The controller in his hand had two sticks projecting upward, which he operated with his thumbs. And on the screen was . . .

. . . a Jaguar XKR zooming around a curve, to the roars of a packed racing stadium!

I nearly meowed out loud as nostalgia gripped me. I pressed forward into the room and jumped onto the boy's bed for a better look. What I wouldn't do for a pair of opposable thumbs!

"Look, Mr. Stink wants to keep you company," the mother said, a bit awkwardly.

The boy, eyes fixed on the screen, did not even glance at me.

"Sure, Mom," he said. "Whatever."

The mother watched the Jaguar tear around a few curves and then said, "That reminds me, I have something you can give the cat. I'll be right back."

She withdrew and shut the door.

Since the boy apparently intended to ignore me, I decided to take the opportunity to explore the room. Stacks of comic books—neat stacks, I had to admit—were piled across the top of a small desk. There were a chair and several bookshelves, also piled with comic books and assorted knickknacks. Posters of spaceships adorned the walls, and the bed was made with dark-blue linens and a quilt with a starry sky theme.

I soon found the source of the peanut butter smell—a discarded, half-eaten sandwich under the bed. I wondered if the mice knew of this room, or if I could barter the information for something to my advantage.

There was another knock at the door, and I heard the mother's voice call out, "Look what else Dad brought home from the store."

I came out from under the bed and saw that the boy

had put down the game controller. He was looking through another Parkside bag.

"I bet Mr. Stink could use a good brushing," the mother was saying.

My ears pricked up.

And then the boy drew something wonderful out of the bag—a brand-new brush!

Now this may sound strange to you, but even though Sir Archibald was a hard-bitten covert operative, he very much enjoyed brushing me on a regular basis. I had not been brushed since he died.

This was no time for dignity. I leaned forward in anticipation. The boy smiled at my eagerness and ran the brush down my back.

I don't think I can adequately explain what it felt like except to say that it was the first time in a long while that I felt . . . *content*.

"Guess you like being brushed, huh cat?" the boy murmured.

If I closed my eyes and flopped on my side, I could almost imagine that I was back in London on a bearskin rug, being brushed by Sir Archibald. A warm fire was roaring, and Sir Archibald had just put a kettle on for tea, and all was right in the world again.

Puuuurrrr.

8

My Great Escape

THE NEXT morning, I accompanied Aaron when he went down to breakfast. It was a perfect opportunity to scout the ground floor for possible escape routes.

At the foot of the stairs was a front hall with a large door and a mail slot. Too small to squeeze through. Off to one side was a sitting room with a garish, gold velvet couch and matching armchairs that did rather scream out to be shredded. They faced a fireplace with a large television set placed inside it.

So much for my dreams of curling up in front of a roaring fire.

Down the hall was the door to the basement stairs

and an unremarkable kitchen with white appliances and wood-veneer cabinets. I longed for the warm, hulking old Aga cooker in Sir Archibald's kitchen. Now that was an appliance a cat could curl up next to for hours at a time.

The boy's mother was standing at the counter, fishing around in her pocketbook, and Aaron was seated at a Formica table in the breakfast nook, eating a bowl of cereal. His sister sat next to him, picking flakes of dry cereal out of her own bowl with her fingers. There was no sign of the father, so I presumed he had left the house already.

"Here you go, kiddo," said the mother, handing her son some money. "That's for lunch. Now remember, I have that interview, so I won't be home after school today. Call me at the paper if you need anything."

Aaron shrugged and shoveled a spoonful of cereal into his mouth. Milk dripped down his chin.

The mother shuffled through some papers in a leather briefcase, obviously not finding whatever she was looking for. She glanced up. "Finish up. You don't want to be late for the bus again." And to herself she added, "Now, where *is* that e-mail?"

She left the room and went upstairs, and Aaron looked down at me.

He picked up his bowl and put it in the sink. Then he glanced at the ceiling and cocked his head at the sounds of his mother pacing around upstairs.

"Okay, shh," Aaron said to me, placing a finger across his lips.

His sister, who was lining up the dry flakes in a row on the edge of the table, looked up.

Aaron withdrew a can from a cupboard and ran it through an electric can opener on the counter. He poured the contents into a bowl from one of the cabinets and placed it on the floor. I sniffed at it.

Fresh tuna in spring water!

"What are you doing?" Lily asked.

"Hurry," he said to me.

"I'll tell Mom."

"Shut up, Lily."

I wolfed down the tuna eagerly and started to lick the stray bits from my lips while Aaron rinsed my bowl out in the sink. Then he gave my head a rough scrub with his damp hand and said, "You're not too bad, Stink. See you after school. Let's go, Lil."

And then Aaron grabbed a backpack from one of the kitchen chairs and headed out the front door while his sister ran to catch up.

He wasn't too bad himself.

★ ★ ★

I was on my way to investigate the rest of the main floor when I heard the mother coming down the stairs.

"Mr. Stink?" she called, and then muttered to herself, "You'd better not be getting into anything."

Sir Archibald had trained in all manner of disguises. Using a rare technique taught to him by Tibetan monks, he could even alter his appearance with muscular control alone. Employing this method, I curled into a flat ball on the floor, tucking my head in so that I appeared to be an area rug. She walked right past me without even noticing.

Now that her back was turned, I made a break for a more secure hiding spot—behind the gold couch.

But the woman must have sensed something, for she spun around and cut me off.

"Oh no you don't, Mr. Stink," she said. "I can't keep an eye on the furniture today, so it's back to the basement for you."

Back to the basement I went.

It was time to pull myself together, take matters into my own paws, and use my training to my advantage. If the mice had found a way into and out of this house, a master counterspy like myself could, too!

I leaped back onto the duct where I had smelled the

fresh air, careful to make no noise this time. I followed it along the ceiling until I was directly above the furnace, where I had encountered Frankie and Vinnie.

The duct disappeared into a high gap in the wall behind the furnace. Around the duct, I could see into a narrow crawl space with less than two feet of clearance. The crawl space apparently covered quite a large area and receded into the darkness in all directions.

I edged inside and soon was prowling the dry dirt floor, smelling the scent of mice and long-dead termites, my eyes wide open and peering into the near-total darkness. This was my natural element: moving silently through the unknown, seeking minute traces of evidence that might be useful to my mission.

A lesser cat might have missed them, but I immediately spotted the faint tracks in the dust. Another animal had been this way some time ago, a rodent of some kind from the shape of the footprints, but clearly larger than a mouse.

I followed the tracks deep into the crawl space until I reached the edge of the house, where the floor joists rested on a crumbling foot-high sill of concrete. A slender shaft of light leaked from under the wall. I took a step back to let my eyes adjust and heard the light crunch of tiny bones.

There, at my paws, was the perfectly articulated skeleton of a small gerbil.

This must be the pet gerbil the boy's mother had mentioned at the Humane Society. No doubt the poor creature had run away from that awful little girl and her sticky hands. I could hardly blame it.

The little thing had been trying to get through a tiny hole that the mice had been using to enter the house. With a few powerful strokes of my front paws and back feet, I enlarged the opening and squeezed through. Just when I thought I was going to be stuck for good, I pressed forward with all my might and felt a rush of fresh air. I breathed deeply and blinked dirt from my eyes, just as a squeaky voice said:

"How 'bout dat, Vinnie! It's a mole dat looks like a cat."

The two mice fell over themselves laughing at me.

"No, lads, it's a cat that looks like a mole." Then I licked my chops and added, "A hungry cat."

They scampered away in terror, and I looked around the side yard.

I was free.

9

A Boy Most Basely Treated

OVER THE next few hours, I developed a fairly good mental map of Woodland Park. But I still had no idea how to get to the airport.

I did learn that my new humans—that is, my jailers—lived in a house near the edge of a large network of residential streets. In London, the humans had enough imagination to give their streets actual names. Here in America, though, many of the streets were simply assigned numbers: North Tenth Avenue, South Tenth Avenue, North Eleventh Avenue, South Eleventh Avenue, and so on.

The houses were of varying size but of uniformly

poor taste. At the far end of Aaron's block, a stoplight controlled the flow of traffic across a six-lane street. A metallic rattling on the other side caught my attention, and I peered more closely, spotting a gray cat jumping onto a rusting blue Dumpster beside a petrol station. I dove for cover behind a large, overflowing rubbish bin, hoping I had not been observed.

Sure enough, it was the lady cat I had seen stealing food from Bruno's dog dish yesterday. But what made me catch my breath was the other cat sitting on the Dumpster with her.

Bugs.

The gray lady cat was glancing around nervously as she said something to him. Bugs lay placidly on his side, his expression unreadable.

Then the little thief caught sight of me peeping around the rubbish bin. Careless. She gasped and scampered off, putting the Dumpster between us.

Bugs and I regarded one another across the six lanes of traffic. My former roommate had not the slightest warmth or affection for me in his eyes. He simply angled his head and proceeded to chew a flea out of the dank fur covering his enormous belly, ignoring me completely.

★ ★ ★

I decided it wouldn't ·hurt to find out if Bruno would help me, despite yesterday's error. After all, he was a local. He would know his way around. I didn't know exactly what I would say to him, and I had little hope he would be cooperative. I did know one thing: an apology would put me at a severe disadvantage. A dog like Bruno would interpret an apology as a sign of weakness.

The enormous mutt was lying in the patchy grass beside his ramshackle doghouse, snoring away. It is always a good policy to let sleeping dogs lie. However, no sooner had I placed a paw on the lawn than his eyes snapped open and he growled. I quickly reached the safety of the roof through a series of impressive leaps.

"Good afternoon, Bruno," I called down brightly. "How was your nap?"

He shook his head and got to his feet. "Get offa my roof," he barked.

"Calm yourself. I don't intend to stay long." I smirked down at him with my chin resting on my paws. "As a matter of fact, if you help me, you will never see me again."

"Now I know why they call you Stink," he finally growled. "I thought I smelled something nasty when I was sleeping."

"I don't smell," I snapped. "It's just a name those humans call me."

Bruno settled back onto his haunches and looked up at me. "Where you from, Stink? You talk funny."

"London, England. And I would be delighted to go back there if you would be so kind as to give me directions to Newark Airport. Do you know how I might find it?"

"Maybe." The dog paused, enjoying his power over me. Finally, he said, "All right, yeah. Yeah I do. I got a coupla cousins over by there in the sanitation industry."

"Junkyard dogs?"

"You could say that."

We studied each other for a few more moments.

"So will you tell me?" I asked.

"What's in it for me?"

"I'd be in your debt, sir."

He laughed and went back to his empty bowl, dragging his heavy chain behind him. "Buzz off. All you cats are the same."

I opened my mouth to respond when an enormous yellow bus pulled to a stop in front of the house. The door opened and children spilled out like ants.

Bruno was off like a shot toward the sidewalk, barking and straining at the end of his chain. The metal stake to which the chain was attached vibrated with the force of his pulling. *Get offa my sidewalk*, he kept repeating. *Move along. This is private property.* Bruno's message was clear in any language, and the young humans scurried away quickly.

Lily was the second person off the bus, and the dog frightened her terribly. She took off down the block toward her house at a run.

Aaron was almost the last one off the bus. Just as he stepped down, a large boy pushed him from behind. Aaron went sprawling across the sidewalk, skinning the heels of his hands. He managed to stop himself at the very edge of the lawn, a mere bite away from Bruno.

Off the grass, punk! Bruno barked at him, leaping forward and getting yanked to his hind legs by the chain. Aaron reeled back against the larger kid who had pushed him.

"Watch it, dork," the kid sneered, pushing him back toward the dog.

Aaron stumbled and cried out, "Quit it, Kyle."

Kyle was heavy and nearly a foot taller than the other children, with greasy bangs and puffy cheeks and a head shaped like a sack of flour.

Two other boys stood nearby, looking uncomfortable.

They were the only ones who had not immediately fled the scene. Kyle threw a sneering smile at them as he grabbed Aaron and hauled him roughly to his feet.

Through the open door, the bus driver called, "Careful there, boys."

"Yes, ma'am," Kyle said, all innocence. "I was just helping him up." He grabbed Aaron's jacket and brushed imaginary dirt from his shoulders with his other hand.

The bus driver eyed all four boys suspiciously but swung the door shut. The bus gave an explosive hiss before pulling away down the block. Kyle didn't even wait until the bus was out of sight before pushing Aaron again, sending him stumbling back.

"'Quit it,'" the bully mimicked in a high, whiny voice. "What are you trying to do, get me in trouble?" Kyle stepped toward Aaron and grabbed the back of his jacket collar, half lifting him off the ground and thrusting him at the dog. "Whatsamatter, don't like dogs, wuss?"

Bruno started barking even louder.

"LET GO!" Aaron shouted, kicking his legs and flailing his arms uselessly at Kyle.

"Ooh, it's a feisty wuss," Kyle laughed, grinning at

the two boys who were watching. "I can't believe you used to be friends with this guy!"

The two boys studied their shoes.

Bruno, egged on by the bully's antics, had become hysterical. *Lemme at him! Lemme at him!* the dog kept repeating, flinging dog drool at Aaron and mixing low growls with ear-shattering barks.

Other dogs in the neighborhood were starting to bark now. *Aw, shut up already, Bruno,* a Labrador complained from a few houses away. *We're trying to sleep.*

"C'mon, Kyle. Let him go," said one of the bystanders. He was a slender Asian boy with short black hair.

"You wanna take his place, Robby?" Kyle dropped Aaron to the sidewalk and advanced on the boy who had spoken up.

Robby held up his hands. "Whoa, Kyle. I'm just saying."

The other kid, a red-haired lad with glasses and an overabundance of freckles, chimed in, "Yeah, Kyle, Robby was just saying, you know, maybe leave Aaron alone for today."

Kyle gave them both a hard look and raised a fist. The boys flinched but held their ground.

"Aw, I'm just playin'. Forget about it, Paul." Kyle let

his fist fly and hit Paul on the shoulder, playfully it seemed, but the boy stumbled back.

"SHUT YER TRAP!" Kyle shouted suddenly at the dog, who stopped barking immediately and lay down.

About time, barked a collie, several blocks away.

"Let's go, you dweebs," Kyle said, and he started down the walk toward the very house I was sitting on. Bruno's house!

The bully—Kyle—was Bruno's boy!

Paul followed the bully reluctantly, giving the dog a wide berth.

Robby was still looking regretfully at Aaron, who was gathering his things and brushing sand out of the scrapes on his palms.

"Well, come on, Robby," Kyle called irritably. "What's *your* problem?"

Aaron looked up at Robby, who glanced away and followed the other two into the house.

I had seen enough.

10

Framed

FOLLOWED AARON as he shuffled home along the sidewalk.

I was torn. On the one paw, I had no reason ever to return to that house again. On the other, I wanted to comfort this boy who had been so kind to me.

But I didn't want his family to know I had an escape route. So when the boy turned up the walk, I went around to the side of the house and entered through the crawl space. I was just rounding the furnace when the little girl opened the basement door.

"Hey, Mr. Stink, wanna play?" she called.

Slipping past her easily, I ran up the stairs into the kitchen. No sign of Aaron.

I paused, sniffing the air. There was something odd about the room, a familiar odor but distinctly out of place.

I shrugged it off and continued on.

Inside the upstairs bathroom, Aaron had removed his jacket and shirt and thrown them onto the floor. He was washing his bloody scrapes and sticking bits of toilet paper to the skin of his palms to stop the bleeding.

Then I noticed something on his back. A bruise. Someone, presumably Kyle, had shoved him against a hard, round object earlier in the day. From the shape and position of the mark on his back, I deduced that the injury had been caused by the combination dial of a school locker. Ouch.

"Great," the boy muttered. "I'm never gonna survive fifth grade."

Poor Aaron.

I knew all too well what the boy was going through. At the French cattery, some of the other kittens had been quite cruel to me, a nameless orphan with no papers or pedigree. I had been teased endlessly and had spent many a night locked outside in the rain by the other kittens, who thought it was a hilarious joke.

Aaron was looking despondently in the mirror.

When life is unfair, sometimes it's helpful to have someone to talk to, even someone who doesn't talk back, so I jumped onto the counter next to him and made my presence known. Sir Archibald had often shared his concerns about ongoing missions with me.

But the boy just looked at me and narrowed his eyes.

"I wanted a dog to protect me. All you do is run away and sleep," he hissed.

My mistake. Wounded animals of all kinds prefer to lick their wounds in private. I jumped back down and went into his room.

A moment later, Aaron crashed into the bedroom, pulled down the shades, and threw himself onto the bed. He burrowed under his comforter like a small, sad animal seeking shelter.

"Why won't everybody just leave me alone?" he said, his voice full of quiet despair.

I walked to the end of the hall and hunkered down at the top of the stairs, folding my legs under me.

The least I could do was keep his sister away.

Before long, I heard the minivan pull into the garage.

"Aaron, I could use some help putting the groceries away," the mother called.

I glanced down the hall toward the boy's room. He didn't respond. He didn't even stir.

"Did you feed Mr. Stink?" the mother called up again. "There's no food in the bowl downstairs."

No food? I hadn't touched the food for fear of cracking a tooth.

I could feel my fur starting to stand on end. Something was not right.

"Aaron!" The mother was beginning to sound irritable now. "You're supposed to feed your cat."

And then she shrieked!

I streaked down the stairs to see what the commotion was. The mother stood in the sitting room, her eyes fiery.

"Mr. Stink! You are a bad, bad cat!" She shook her finger at me. "Bad cat!"

"Bad cat!" Lily repeated, giggling.

"Very bad cat! No dinner for you!" the mother continued, pointing.

I looked around in bewilderment. And then I saw.

The upholstered arms of the gold velvet sofa had been shredded!

Yellow chunks of foam stuffing bulged through the

ragged gashes like guts from a maimed caterpillar. The work was clearly that of a cat. But I had not committed the dastardly deed.

I had been framed!

11

I Am Cruelly Tortured

DINNER THAT night was a tense affair. The mother was furious about the couch, and Aaron was very quiet after his encounter with Bruno's boy, Kyle. The only two who seemed to be having a normal day were Lily and the father.

"Didn't you interview somebody big today, or something, honey?" the father said cheerily in a brave attempt to lighten the mood.

I was sitting on the bay windowsill in the kitchen, tucked behind a large, rather ratty-looking potted plant. The mother had tried to lock me in the basement again, but I had been eluding her successfully by staying out of sight. I was troubled by the boy's situation.

How long had Bruno's boy been torturing him?

The mother smiled grudgingly at her husband. "Let's just say a certain public official probably won't be getting reelected when I write this one up."

The parents met each other's gaze, and then both glanced at Aaron, who was staring unhappily at his plate. Beside him, his sister was eating peas one by one with her fingers.

Silence descended upon the table again like a Siberian winter.

"So I brought home some really nice wet food for Mr. Stink today," the father tried again. "It's all-organic. Neat, huh?"

I wrinkled my nose. All-organic? What exactly was that supposed to mean?

"Because your mother found that can of tuna in the trash, you know," the father continued.

The boy looked up, stricken.

"It's okay. I'm sure he needed a treat. That cat's had a rough time, I bet."

They didn't know the half of it.

"But let's give him cat food from now on, all right?" the father said. "People food is bad for cats."

This was news to me.

The boy was pushing his food around his plate. The

afternoon's scrapes had left a wicked set of scabs on the heels of his hands.

"What happened to your hands, Aaron?" the father asked, concern in his voice.

"Recess," he mumbled. "I fell."

His mother and father looked at each other again. From where I was sitting, it was obvious they didn't buy it.

The mother tried a new topic. "What you should get that cat is a scratching post."

"No kidding. But we need to train him too. We can't expect him to know what we want unless we reward him for good behavior and punish him for things like scratching the sofa," the father said. "Cats are perfectly trainable, no matter what people say."

Let them try. Their brainwashing techniques would not work on me.

"Aaron, maybe you and your dad can train Mr. Stink together," the mother said. "I don't want any more furniture scratched up."

Something was not right here. I was having the same feeling I had had that night in Sir Archibald's townhouse. Who had done this to me and to these innocent humans? And why?

I went to investigate the damage for which I was

being blamed. Judging from the spacing between the rents in the fabric, the cat responsible had smaller paws than mine. Much smaller. Quite dainty, in fact.

Any doubts I might have had as to the identity of the criminal were dispelled when I stole down to the basement to investigate my now-empty bowl of dry food.

Short gray hairs were stuck to the inside of the bowl.

All evidence pointed in one direction.

I left the house immediately and took a tour of the lady gray cat's known haunts. Bruno's food dish. The blue Dumpster. But I did not see her or Bugs, and I had no obvious leads to pursue. Besides, it was dark out, and getting cold. I snuck back into the family's house and warmed up on a heating register while I pondered what to do next.

I was back in London. The parlor was warm, a cheery fire was roaring in the grate, and a bowl of cream had been set out for me. Outside, I heard the soft sound of falling rain. It was all so wonderfully familiar. And then I heard a strange noise. A sort of choking sound. I looked up and saw—

Sir Archibald choking on a biscuit!

He flailed wildly in my direction, hands around his throat.

My heart slammed in my chest when I saw his face—or, rather, his lack of face! His face was a blur. A blank!

I couldn't remember what my dear Sir Archibald's face looked like!

I woke with a start, breathless, only to find the little girl hovering over me.

"You snore, Mr. Stink!" Lily giggled at me.

I blinked my eyes open blearily. The room lights were on, and something was scratching at my neck. I craned my head around to lick at the annoyance, only to discover that someone had tied a bow—a *pink* bow—around my head while I slept.

Now, I can understand how humans, ignorant as they are, could be oblivious to certain basic facts about anatomy. But even *were* I female, the bubblegum-pink organdy bow would have been in hideous taste. Was this some kind of evil torture? It wasn't just the bow that was embarrassing; it was the thought that I had allowed the little girl to get the drop on me.

Then I looked down and saw the tutu.

Trust me, you would have lost your temper too. Immediately, I was on my feet. The sight amused her greatly, nearly sending the little girl into hysterics.

"Lily?" her father called from another room. "What are you up to?"

"Now hold still," she laughed, tears streaming from her eyes. As she reached toward me, I saw that she held in her hands a pair of pink ballet slippers. Clearly, she intended to tie these over my paws.

Enough was enough.

I backed into a corner, hissing in warning and ruffling my fur. If I do say so myself, I present a particularly fierce aspect when I ruffle my fur.

But the idiot child only laughed harder. She continued to press forward with her ridiculous ballet shoes. I hissed more loudly and growled low in my chest.

"Lily, stop torturing that cat," the father called again, but he did not come to my rescue. Why didn't someone *do* something? Where was Aaron?

"C'mere, kitty kitty," the girl said, wiggling the shoes at me.

Well, I had warned her.

I extended my claws and struck like lightning, intending to frighten her and, with luck, shred those awful shoes to bits.

But my weeks of confinement had thrown off my usually expert timing. I caught her full on the arm, leaving a set of angry red scratch marks behind.

She looked down at her wound in disbelief.

And then screamed!

Before I could turn around, I was in a cage, pink tutu and all.

12

A Fate Worse than Death

THE CAGE was dropped roughly back in the laundry room by the boy's father. He closed the door firmly, plunging the room into semidarkness.

I squirmed around in the small cat carrier, which smelled of new plastic. Another recent arrival from the pet store, no doubt. The drab beige walls seemed to be closing in around me, pressing in more and more tightly. The air rapidly grew stuffy, despite the grillwork door on one side. Surely they didn't intend to leave me in here?

(Even a master spy has to have a secret weakness. Mine, I'm afraid, is a touch of claustrophobia.)

I took a deep breath and twisted out of the detestable tutu and bow. Past experience had taught me that a few well-placed kicks at the corners might dislodge the spring-loaded pins of the door. However, this particular locking mechanism was solidly built, and all my efforts earned me was a pair of sore feet.

Always coming up with something new, these humans.

I studied the problem carefully: I had not trained myself to be an expert lockpick only to be thwarted by something so ridiculously simple. I pressed a paw against the gaps in the grillwork near the lock, but the holes were too small to fit more than the very tip through. If only I had something I could pass through the . . . wait. The tutu!

My claws made short work of the fabric, and soon I had fashioned a narrow loop, which I pushed through one of the holes in the door. Delicately maneuvering the pink taffeta with the sharp tips of my claws, I managed to wind it around the two prongs that controlled the spring pins. Who needs thumbs, anyway?

I yanked the free end with my teeth, twisting to push against the door at the same time. The door sprang open, and I nearly tumbled out onto the floor.

Freedom!

I've still got it, I thought to myself. I leaped down and took a deep breath of the detergent-tinged air of the laundry room.

And then I heard the voices on the other side of the door.

". . . be okay. Sure, there might be a scar, but look, consider it a lesson well learned. Animals are not toys," the father was saying, and I couldn't have agreed more.

"Howard! I can't believe you'd say that! She could have been seriously injured."

"Could have been, but . . ."

"No, it doesn't matter. We should take that cat to the vet and have him declawed."

Her words echoed in the crawl space for a moment. *Declawed!*

I had heard of such barbaric practices from the common cats of London's back alleyways and fish markets. For those who have never been exposed to the darker aspects of human society, declawing is a procedure in which the last joint of each toe is removed by a disreputable butcher in some filthy back room. Since a cat's claw is really just the nail growing out of this joint, the claws are unable to grow back.

In other words, they wanted to chop off the ends of my toes!

"Declawed?" the father said at last. "That's cruel."

"He'll get over it. Think of Lily. Not to mention the couch!"

A new voice caught my attention.

"Mom? Dad?"

"Aaron?" The mother sighed. "We were just discussing what to do about that cat of yours."

"We're talking about having him declawed," the father added, "unless you can convince us you'll keep a closer eye on him. We don't want any repeats of today."

The boy cleared his throat. "Well, I wanted to talk to you about Mr. Stink, too."

I pricked my ears up. Was the boy going to defend me?

The Feline Code of Honor requires that a cat of breeding never abandon his or her human to danger, but I had no idea if such a code existed among humans. Certainly, Sir Archibald had never let me down.

"The thing is," the boy began.

Go on, boy, I wanted to shout. *You can do it! Tell them not to chop my toes off!*

"The thing is, you were right, Mom. I'm not ready to take care of a cat. After he gets declawed, you can give him to Lily. Whatever you want, I don't care." And then I heard him run upstairs.

The words rang in my ears. *I don't care.*

Despite myself, I felt my heart sink. To think that I had actually expected the boy to defend me. But no, I was nothing to him. What honor was there in staying with a boy who didn't even want my companionship? Who was quite happy to send me away to have my toes chopped off?

I recalled the fate of the mummified gerbil. That was it. I was leaving this dungeon of horrors for good! I headed for the tunnel.

"All right, listen, honey," I heard the father say. "If you still feel the same after I get back from Chicago, I'll take Mr. Stink to get declawed. It's only a couple of days."

I paused. Chicago?

If memory served correct, Chicago was quite a distance from New Jersey. And that meant . . .

"Oh, I forgot to tell you," the mother was saying. "They moved my meeting at the paper to seven A.M. tomorrow. Can you drive yourself to the airport and just leave your car in the lot?"

The airport!

In our darkest hours, so are our fortunes sometimes reversed.

I turned around and went back to the laundry room.

I could barely contain myself. I would stow away in the father's car and get chauffeured directly to the airport. What could be more perfect?

So long, New Jersey! Ta-ta, cheerio, and all that.

13

The Getaway

HAD DIFFICULTY falling asleep, consumed as I was with excitement over my upcoming trip.

How exactly was I going to slip past customs and onto a plane bound for Norway? Could I, perhaps, bribe another animal to trade places with me? Or could I sneak in among the human passengers and enjoy the trip in relative comfort?

Sometime near midnight, I finally dropped off. And dreamed of beluga caviar and crème fraiche falling to the carpeted floor of the first-class cabin.

I awoke to the sound of someone creeping down the basement stairs. I bounded over to the dryer and climbed into the cage, pulling the door partway closed behind me.

Light spilled into the room. "Mr. Stink, are you awake?" the boy called quietly. He was wearing pajamas.

My internal clock told me it was well after midnight. What was he doing up?

He approached the cage carefully, and I saw what he was up to: he was holding my brush. "Hey there, Mr. Stink," he said.

He opened the cage door and peered in. I regarded him coldly.

"Wanna get brushed?" he asked. Obviously, he was feeling bad about his betrayal and wanted to soothe his own guilt.

Tempting. But I would not oblige him. I turned my back and hunkered down.

He stood there for a few more moments, and then he gave up and went upstairs. I closed my eyes and went back to sleep.

Before the sun was even up the next morning, the mother came through the laundry room and deposited a bowl of wet cat food next to my water dish, making a small disgusted noise when I did not immediately run over and start eating. She went into the garage, fired up the minivan, and was gone.

Luck was on my side, for I saw that the mother had not closed the door tightly. I could easily sneak into the garage now.

First, however, I strolled over to the food, which glistened in the bowl, moist with gravy. You may wonder how I could think about food at such a time, but a spy is well advised to eat when he can. Besides, I was hungry.

I gave the meal a few experimental sniffs, then touched the tip of my tongue to the very top of the food.

Delectable!

Perhaps delectable is stretching it a bit. But it certainly was a tolerable liver-and-chicken pâté. Rather a good beginning to my last day in Woodland Park.

After licking the bowl clean and carefully washing my face, I squeezed my way into the garage, flipping the door shut behind me with a back foot.

Since the convertible top of the father's MGB was up, I hid in the shadows beneath the low chassis of the sports car. A moment later, the door swung open and the father stumbled through the doorway with a large suitcase in each hand. One suitcase was shoved into the MGB's small trunk. The other was jammed into the small space behind the front seats.

The father went back inside, and I took the opportunity to leap through the open door on the driver's side. I crouched on the floor beneath the passenger seat, making sure my tail was coiled out of view. The gap beneath the seat was very small, and I could barely fit.

The father reappeared and climbed into the car, setting a briefcase on the floor of the passenger side. I heard the click of the garage door opener, the clattering of the great door rising open, then the fat thrum of the MGB's engine starting.

Newark Airport, here I come!

I didn't expect the boy to get in. Much less sit on top of me.

He flung himself into the passenger seat and slammed the door, and the bottom of the seat pressed down on me. A pair of smelly sneakers swung into view.

And these people had the audacity to call *me* Mr. Stink?

"This is the fourth time you've missed the bus this month," the boy's father finally said, once we had been under way for a few minutes.

The boy said nothing.

"I—" the father started to say. But he stopped and took a deep breath.

The rest of the car ride passed in thunderous silence. As if in sympathy, the skies overhead were dark and cloudy, threatening rain.

At last, the car pulled up a long, curved drive and stopped. I could hear schoolyard laughter and the shouts of children outside the car.

"Okay, out you go," the boy's father said, his cheerful voice sounding a little forced to my ears. "I'll see you in a few days."

The boy opened the door without saying a word and started to get out.

"They always give away cool stuff at these pet food conferences," the father tried again. "I'll bring you back something to cheer you up, all right? One of those caps with the dog ears?"

The boy was reaching back into the car for his book bag. "Okay, thanks."

"Uh, Aaron?"

"Yeah?"

"You know, if someone is giving you trouble, I can call his father if you want."

"That'd just make everything worse," the boy said glumly, and slammed the car door.

His father rolled down the passenger window and shouted after him. "I'll be back on Wednesday. Your mom has the hotel number, all right? You can always call me."

Aaron kept walking.

Just as his father was about to pull out, his cell phone rang. He shoved the stick into neutral and set the parking brake. "Howard Green," he said into the phone.

Outside the car, I heard a familiar voice sneer, "Well if it isn't the little scaredy-cat himself."

Ignoring the risk of discovery, I jumped onto the suitcase behind the front seats and put my paws against the side of the convertible top. Through a clear plastic porthole, I could see the boy climbing a long flight of stairs leading up to the main entrance of the school.

"That sounds fine," the father was saying. "Sure, I'll try to pick up a case from the booth in Chicago."

A crowd had gathered to watch the spectacle.

Kyle, the tough-looking thug, pushed the boy hard in the back, sending him stumbling, the strap of his backpack slipping off his shoulder. The crowd of kids laughed. The other two boys, Robby and Paul, hung back uncomfortably as Kyle tormented their former friend.

My sensitive ears picked up what Kyle was saying.

"Duh, walk much, Aar-head?"

And then he started barking at Aaron like a dog. The boy flinched away and glanced back at the car, his face a mask of fear.

His father saw none of this. " 'Bye," he said into the phone. Then he put it away and shifted the car into gear. As the car pulled off, I could just barely hear the bully's parting threat.

"See you at recess, scaredy-cat."

The boy's eyes were small black pits of despair. He hunched his shoulders and filed into the school like a prisoner going to his execution.

I watched him until he disappeared.

With every block the car drove, I felt my stomach grow tighter and my tail stiffer.

I couldn't get the image of the boy's face out of my mind. Especially the eyes.

A low rumbling rolled across the sky, and the first few fat drops of rain began to strike the windshield.

I tried to convince myself that I didn't care what the boy was going through. The boy certainly didn't care about me. Why, he was quite happy to have me maimed and then presented as a plaything to his horrible sister!

But with each squeak of the windshield wiper blades, a feeling rose in me, a feeling I knew all too well.

Something about this boy—perhaps his stoic bravery in the face of a foe twice his size, or maybe the grudging warmth in his wide brown eyes as he had brushed me—whatever it was, it reminded me of Sir Archibald, and I knew deep in my heart that, like it or not, I was honor bound to help him.

I had failed Sir Archibald. I would not fail this boy. The airport could wait. There was time enough to find Sir Archibald's killer. Somehow, I knew my old human would approve of my actions.

After all, a cat without honor is no cat at all.

"Terrific," the father muttered from the front seat. "I'm almost out of gas."

The car abruptly pulled into a petrol station, and an attendant ran up, ducking his head against the rain.

"Fill 'er up with regular," Mr. Green said. "I'm gonna run inside and grab a coffee." He scrambled out hastily, leaving the door ajar. I stared at the crack, my tail thumping.

Once. Twice.

And then I was off.

14

Back to the Scene of the Crime

AND THAT is how I came to be in the middle of the street in a torrential downpour, blinded by the headlights of an oncoming car as my nine lives flashed before my eyes.

There was no way I could leap out of the way in time.

Now, you may be thinking, why not simply crouch down and let the car pass over me? But I knew too much about cars, and I had seen ignorant street cats try it in London, with tragic results.

I really had just one option, and I had to time it perfectly. Just before impact, I leaped onto the bonnet of the car, then the roof, and then I was over it and back on the street. For one brief moment I glimpsed the driver, his mouth wide open in astonishment. A squeal of tires on the slick road surface and a metallic crunch echoed behind me as I completed my dash across the road.

I rewarded myself with a quick glance over my shoulder. No fewer than eight cars had skidded to a complete stop, blocking traffic in both directions, but luckily no one appeared hurt. I could see the boy's father on the other side of the road, drinking his coffee and scratching his head as he looked at the mess in the street.

It took the better part of the day to work my way back home. By the time I turned down the boy's block, the rain had stopped, it was growing dark, and I was thoroughly wet—a state no cat enjoys.

Still, I had a mission to accomplish, and the sooner the better.

In no time, I found exactly what I was looking for: a half-empty bag of charcoal briquettes left on someone's porch. Scrambling into the bag, I covered my wet fur with a thick coat of black dust. It was a perfect disguise—I would be impossible to spot in the shadows,

and my scent would be concealed as well.

Time for a stakeout.

As soon as Bruno's house came into view, I crouched low to the ground and scanned the yard. The enormous dog was sitting in front of his house watching the street with cold, flinty eyes. Invisible under my black coat, I stole silently through the bushes until I was as close to the house as I dared, then settled down to see what I could learn.

I could sit perfectly still for hours, eyes mere slits, appearing almost asleep, and yet completely alert and ready for action at a moment's notice. As an unofficial MI9 operative, I had patiently outwaited jewel thieves and kidnappers at Sir Archibald's side.

After an hour or so, the front door opened, and Kyle came out of the house, carrying a dog dish with food. Paul and Robby trailed behind him.

"You got any new games, Paul?" Kyle was saying. "We could go to your house."

"A couple," Paul said guardedly.

"You know," Robby cut in, "Aaron has that new racing game. It's awesome."

Kyle cut him off. "I decide who we hang out with. And it's not that dweeb."

"Sorry," Robby mumbled.

Abruptly, Kyle's mood shifted. "Hey, forget about it. Watch this." He placed the dog dish on the ground and whistled. "C'mere, boy. Dinner!"

Bruno stood and trotted over to the food. Just as he was about to reach the dish, his chain snapped taut and he lunged to a stop, an inch short of his meal. He strained a few more times, then lay down on the ground and looked up at Kyle submissively.

Kyle laughed uproariously. "Isn't that hilarious? He never learns." He elbowed the other two boys, but Robby and Paul weren't laughing. Kyle scowled. "Aw, c'mon. Let's go."

He continued to snicker as they disappeared down the block.

"Why do you let your boy torture you that way?" I asked quietly from the shadows.

Bruno's head snapped around, and he focused on the bushes where I was hidden.

He shrugged. "Hey, I gotta eat."

"Doesn't seem to be helping you much," I said pointedly.

Then a flash of yellow eyes in the dark caught my attention.

"Shh," I warned and faded deeper into the bushes. "We've got company."

Bruno squinted suspiciously in my direction, then closed his eyes and pretended to sleep.

A patch of gray fur seemed to detach itself from the darkness of the street, and I watched the young thief slink into the yard with the casual ease of a professional. She was still cute, in a rough but charming sort of way. She hesitated a few feet from Bruno's bowl and studied the dog carefully, staying well beyond the reach of his chain.

Bruno began to snore lightly.

At that, she approached and stuck her head right into his bowl, shoveling food into her mouth. She never even saw me coming. I leaped out of the shadows and landed on top of her, scattering food everywhere.

The young lady hissed furiously.

"My, my," I said, holding her down easily with one large paw. "That is no way for a lady to speak."

"I ain't no lady and let me go," she said.

Bruno opened his eyes and sat up.

"Aw no," she groaned. "You're in this together?"

"I'm asking the questions," I said sternly. I had witnessed interrogations in the MI9 basement many times. "First off, what is your name?"

"My name? My name is— GET OFF ME!" She

lashed out with a back foot, but I had seen it coming. Her feet connected with thin air.

"Nice try," I drawled. "Name?"

"Kitty," she said quietly.

I couldn't help but snicker. "How very original." Bruno snorted.

Her features hardened. "For your information, it's short for Katerina. It was my grandmother's name, so don't give me any guff about it."

Touché. Even a common street cat knew her pedigree better than I knew mine.

"Well, Kitty," I said, "do you want to tell me why you broke into my house?" Bruno cocked his head at me, but I shot him a look and he held his tongue.

"How do you know that was me?" she said defiantly.

"Never mind how. Did Bugs put you up to it?"

Her eyes widened in fear. "Bugsy? You leave my brother alone. He ain't done nuttin'!"

Ah, so they were brother and sister. That explained their meeting.

"Then who put you up to it?" I demanded.

"Nobody put me up to it. I was hungry. When Bugsy's out, I gotta work twice as hard. He's too big to feed himself on his own."

That I could believe. "I don't care about the food."

I pressed down on her with my paws. "Why did you scratch up the couch?"

"I can't breathe! I'll tell you!" I eased up, and she took a deep breath. "Okay, this cat came up to me the other night. Big fella. Told me to go in and scratch up all the furniture. Eating your food was my idea."

"What did he look like?"

"I . . . I never saw his face. He was big, bigger than you. And . . . and he had a funny accent!"

Strange. "Like mine? British?"

"Not funny like yours. I can't explain it."

"Anything else?"

"That's all I know, honest."

I glanced at Bruno. He nodded.

"All right," I continued. "I believe you owe this gentleman an apology for stealing his food."

"Yeah, you owe me an apology," Bruno growled.

"I don't owe nobody nuttin'," she said, managing to sound indignant.

"Then I'm afraid you'll have to make up for all the food you've stolen some other way. Hey, Bruno, do you want the front half or the back half?"

Bruno licked his chops, grinning at me as he understood my meaning. "You pick."

"Awright, awright! Sorry," she said, not sounding

the least bit sorry.

"Well done," I said. "I am going to release you now, and you are never going to steal from Mr. Bruno again, do you take my meaning?"

"He means 'Or else,'" Bruno added helpfully.

She nodded, her face sullen. I lifted my paw, and she scrambled away without a backward glance.

"Women," I said.

Bruno and I looked at each other and laughed. I nosed his food bowl closer, and he took a few hungry bites and then looked up at me.

"I owe you one," he said gruffly.

I studied my claws. "There is one thing you can do for me, actually."

"Name it."

"It's about your boy and his behavior at the bus stop," I said.

Bruno lifted an ear. "You mean the way he beats up on your boy?"

I almost said, *He's not my boy.* But it was simpler just to say, "That's right. Can you help me put a stop to it?"

The dog looked uncomfortable. "Look, I know you cats got a code and stuff. We got one too. You protect the leader of the family, you guard his stuff—that's how it works. If he gets mean, well, it's not up to me to question," he said helplessly. "I just can't go against the family."

I couldn't help but admire his sense of loyalty, however misplaced.

"Of course," I said after a pause. "Thank you for your time."

I turned and padded away.

"Hey, Stink," Bruno called.

"Yes?"

"You didn't hear it from me, but you might wanta check out our basement." Then he purposely turned his back to me.

"The basement?"

"Funny," Bruno said to the air. "I coulda swore I heard a cat. But there's no one here."

"Thanks," I whispered.

"Smell ya later, Stink."

I sighed.

15

The Plan Unfolds

BRUNO'S BASEMENT was simple enough to break into—the humans had left a window open a crack, which I was able to slither through.

The basement was filthy, with a crumbling concrete floor and bric-a-brac crammed floor to ceiling—old furniture, magazines, broken television sets. I wrinkled my nose and jumped to the floor. Immediately, something cold and sticky oozed between my toes.

Both my front paws had landed in glue traps, those horrible little plastic squares of glue used by humans to kill mice. I looked around the basement in shock. Hundreds of mousetraps of all descriptions covered every inch of the floor!

Someone, it seemed, had a thing about mice.

"The big dumb kid? Oh, sure, we know him," Vinnie said. "Bad news, dat one."

Frankie chimed in. "My grandpa, Frankie Senior? He grew up in dat house, back when da kid was still in diapers. Little brat used to collect tails. I ain't kiddin'. Tails! Look real close next time you see him. He got a big scar on his nose where my grandma bit him one time."

Vinnie laughed. "Yeah, she made an impression all right. Now he sees one of us, he runs da udder way."

"Can't stand da sight of mice," Frankie added.

"Which explains the traps," I mused.

Vinnie sighed wistfully. "Nobody works dat house for scrap now . . . too risky."

I mulled this over, a plan already forming in my head. "What if I wanted to hire you for a job?"

"A job? It'd cost ya," Vinnie said craftily.

"Yeah, we don't work cheap!" Frankie piped in. "Specially not for cats."

"I'm quite prepared to pay," I said. "But I think I shall require more than two of you. Do you have any family?"

"Family?" Vinnie squeaked. "We got cousins all over dis neighborhood!"

"How many cousins?" I asked.

"Oh, we got a *lotta* cousins. Whatcha got in mind?"

I smiled.

It began simply enough. Every day before the postman arrived, I would sneak out and stand on the front stoop.

"You're just like a dog, you are," the postman would say, patting me on the head before he put the mail through the mail slot.

While I distracted him, one or two mice would sneak into his mailbag and chew their way into some of Kyle's mail. A mail-order CD. A magazine in a plastic sleeve. A box of cookies from his grandmother.

This continued for several days before the first intelligence reports reached me.

"Yeah, he's pretty freaked out," Vinnie said, snickering. "He won't open da mail no more."

"More," I said coldly.

"You got it, boss."

The mice escalated their efforts. Soon, Kyle was finding mice in his shoes, in his schoolbags, in his bedclothes, even in his breakfast cereal.

The mice were beside themselves with glee.

"I tell ya, dat house is a gold mine!" Vinnie said. "It ain't been picked over for food in years. We're gonna be rich, even on top of da fee you promised us, Mr. Stink."

"More," I told them again.

The whole neighborhood heard Kyle scream early the next morning when he put on his underwear.

The morning of the grand finale, I tried to eat my food and act as normal as possible. But when Aaron and his sister left the house for school, I slipped out the escape tunnel and followed them from a safe distance. The boy shuffled down the street toward the bus stop, clearly dreading the daily encounter with Kyle.

But when the bus pulled up, Kyle was nowhere to be seen. Bruno was sitting placidly on the front lawn, eyeing the crowd of schoolkids suspiciously. The doors popped open, and the kids started to file on, one by one. Aaron looked up, relief clear on his face.

The bus driver peered out. "Where's Kyle? He sick?"

One or two kids shrugged.

The bus driver honked her horn, which brought Bruno to his feet.

"Hey, Kyle," she shouted out the door. "You're gonna miss the bus."

The front door opened a crack, and Kyle stuck his head out, looking pale. He shook slightly as he scanned the ground outside, then dashed frantically down the walk to the bus stop. When he caught sight of Aaron, though, Kyle recovered his old swagger.

"Hey, look, it's my favorite scaredy-cat," Kyle sneered, and Aaron visibly deflated. "Hand it over."

Aaron looked at him stubbornly. "I don't have any lunch money today."

Kyle took a menacing step, and Aaron gave up and shoved his backpack at him.

"Thanks!" Kyle said with a mean smile. "Let's see what we have here, shall we?" He flipped open the knapsack, dug around inside, and pulled out a brown-paper lunch bag. "How sweet, Mommy packed a bag lunch today?"

A few of the other kids snickered, gathering around.

"Everyone get on the bus. Now! Or I'm leaving without you," the bus driver shouted from her seat.

Kyle ignored her. He stuck his hand into Aaron's

lunch and pulled out a small plastic bag with a chocolate cupcake inside.

"Excellent," he said. "I just love cupcakes."

He lowered his mouth to take a bite when out of the cupcake popped Vinnie. The mouse took a flying leap at the thug, landed on his shoulder, and then quickly scampered into his jacket.

"Get it offa me!" Kyle squeaked, clearly hysterical, sounding like a mouse himself. The other kids watched in stunned silence as he screamed and ripped off his jacket, stomping down on it. Vinnie dodged Kyle's feet easily and ran toward me.

Now came my big moment. I strolled out of the bushes calmly and picked the mouse up gently in my mouth.

"Hey, it's Mr. Stink," Lily said from the bus, her fingers gripping the edge of an open window.

"Look, even that cat has more guts than Kyle," someone said, laughing.

"Yeah, what a chicken."

Soon, all the kids began to laugh and make chicken sounds: "Bwak! Bwak! Bwak! Kyle's afraid of mi-ice! Kyle's afraid of mi-ice!"

"I am *not*!" Kyle said angrily.

I took a step in his direction, dangling Vinnie from

my mouth, and Kyle quailed.

"*Boo!*" the mouse squeaked, sticking out his tongue.

Kyle turned and fled back into his house.

When I looked back, Aaron was staring at me through the window of the bus.

16

Pardoned

DEPOSITED VINNIE in front of the storm drain where he and his cousin Frankie lived. The other mouse came out to greet us.

"Good news, Vinnie," Frankie reported. "I just got word from da fence. Dat baloney's gonna be a piece a cake to move."

In payment for a job well done, I had promised Vinnie and Frankie an entire package of bologna, filched during the night from the kitchen. I regretted stealing, but it seemed a small price to pay for the boy's dignity.

Vinnie kicked his paws in delight. "We're gonna be rich!"

"So long, Woodland Park."

"Hello, Staten Island," they said in unison.

The two mice high-fived each other and rolled in the gutter, laughing.

"Nice doin' business with ya, Stink!" they called after me.

So long, Woodland Park, indeed.

Now that my work here was finished, it was time for me to think about how I was going to make my way to

the airport. Sir Archibald's killer was still at large.

I trotted around to the side yard and approached the entrance to the escape tunnel.

"And just where have you been, cat? I've been looking for you all morning."

The boy's mother was standing behind me, hands on her hips. I sat back on my haunches and tried to look up at her apologetically.

She glared at me for a few more moments, but then softened. As I may have mentioned, I do have a way with women.

"Well, come on then," she said, going around to the back of the house. She opened a screen door off the kitchen and held it open for me. "In or out."

I trotted briskly into the house to find the boy's father seated at the kitchen table. He had apparently just returned from his trip to Chicago.

"So I called the Humane Society to schedule an appointment for declawing," he said, "and they said since I was at the airport, I might want to stop over at cargo. Apparently they got our cat from the lost-luggage department and they still had his carrier. Seems Mr. Stink is British. Who knew?"

The carrier was sitting on a chair next to him. I jumped inside and inhaled deeply. My carrier! It was the only solid thing I had left to remember London by. And Sir Archibald.

The baggage tags were still on it, and I could even smell faint traces of Miss Astrid's perfume . . . and something else. Something very strange indeed. (When your nose is as sensitive as mine, detecting such things is second nature, and I had spent years perfecting my skills at smell profiling.)

"Aw, look. He's homesick," the mother said, making herself a cup of coffee. "He doesn't look like a British cat."

"What's a British cat supposed to look like?"

The mother shrugged and laughed. "I don't know. Stuffy?"

I looked closely at the tags. They had been altered! Instead of EVE, the code for the airport in Evenes, Norway, they appeared to read EWR, the code for Newark, New Jersey.

Even stranger was how they had been altered—not with ink, but with a carefully etched network of fine scratch marks. It was the work of an insane genius. I looked more closely.

There was no mistaking it—these marks had been made by the claws of a *cat*.

I reeled back in shock.

Suddenly the pieces fell together. The altered baggage tags. The mysterious cat who had hired Kitty. The familiar voices I had heard talking during my tranquilizer-induced stupor. Even getting me declawed had been part of his plan.

A human spy was not responsible for Sir Archibald's death. It had been a cat all along!

But who was it? I had made more than one enemy in my time as an unofficial MI9 operative. Doctor Strangepaw. Mi Yow the Merciless. Don Catleone. And I had heard that the dreaded Klaws was on the loose. It could be any one of them.

One thing was clear: this mystery cat had orchestrated everything with shocking precision. My coming to America had been no baggage mix-up. I had been sent here deliberately.

Which meant that Sir Archibald's killer was not in Norway.

He was right here. In New Jersey.

I was still reeling from this discovery when Aaron and Lily came home from school. The boy was in noticeably better spirits.

"Hey, sport," the mother said. "How was school?"

"Pretty good," the boy said, and from the expression

on his mother's face, it was clear that it hadn't been "pretty good" for a long time. "How's the cat?"

His mother frowned. "He was gone all day. I thought he'd run away."

"He wouldn't do that," the boy said, looking at me. "He's a good cat."

His mother laughed. "A good cat? He's a fighter. I bet he'll rip every stick of furniture we own to shreds, just to keep those claws of his sharp."

The boy glanced uncomfortably at me and then said, "Mom, if I promise to watch him and make sure he doesn't scratch anything, can we not declaw him?"

"What?"

"Well, he's obviously an outdoor cat, you know? And if he doesn't have any claws, he won't be able to stand up for himself. You know, like Bruno's a really mean dog," he said in a persuasive voice.

The mother looked doubtful.

"Please, Mom? If I promise to take care of him?"

"You already promised me you'd take care of him."

"Yeah, but I mean it this time."

She raised her eyebrows at the boy, and the boy looked back at her very seriously. "I really mean it."

She sighed, and I wanted to dance for joy!

"You're going to need to come up with a name for

him. You can't keep letting us call him Mr. Stink."

He looked at me and I squeezed my eyes shut, willing him to pick something more dignified, something more befitting an international cat of mystery.

"Mr. Stink's okay," he said with a grin. "It kinda grows on you."

I groaned inwardly.

Aaron found me napping on the warm clothes dryer. Of course, it wasn't as elegant as my thick velvet bed at Sir Archibald's, but there was something comfortable about falling asleep to the rhythmic thumping.

"So, uh, we're not going to have you declawed after all," Aaron said.

I blinked up at him.

The boy reached out a tentative hand as if to pet me, and then, as if thinking the better of it, started to pull his hand back. Instead, he gave me a dignified nod and turned to go. At the door he paused and looked back to me.

And then the boy, *my boy*, said, "By the way. Thanks."

I flicked my tail.

17

A Calling Card

THE ROUTINE of American suburban life soon grew quite pleasant, especially after the family installed an access panel for me in the back door of their house. As a newly dubbed "indoor/outdoor" cat, I could perform my duties much more easily.

My first order of business was to track down my unknown adversary. I described a number of my more fearsome enemies to Kitty.

"I didn't get a good look at him, but I'm pretty sure he didn't have a glass eye. Or a metal paw. And what kind of cat wears a scarf anyway?"

I sighed.

"No, the only funny thing about him was his

accent," she continued. "And I think he was missing part of an ear. And his fur was kinda long. And he was big. Real big. No-neck big."

"So you didn't get a good look at him?" I asked dryly.

Kitty's description matched half of the street cats in New Jersey. But for his accent, he sounded like a garden-variety local thug. It was not enough to go on.

Having reached a dead end, all I could do was keep an eye on my family. They were my responsibility now. Because of this, I made it a habit to walk Aaron to the bus stop every morning. This was also a useful deterrent in case Kyle got up to his old tricks. Paul and Robby joined us most mornings.

"Hey, Aaron," Robby said as he and Paul crossed the street to join us. "My mom said I could stay over tonight."

"I'm in too," Paul said.

"Cool," Aaron said. "Guess what game I just got?"

Aaron was a completely different boy now, happy. And the other boys weren't scared to be friends with him anymore.

When Kyle came out of the house and saw me, he shot me a dirty look. Aaron snickered and winked at me. "See ya after school, Stink."

Bruno walked over as far as his chain would reach. "Hey, Stink, check it out. I got a new roof."

Sure enough, Bruno's doghouse had a shiny new tin roof and a bright coat of paint. And there was fresh water and food.

"Let me guess," I said. "Kyle wants you to keep the mice away?"

The dog nodded. "Things sure do smell a whole lot different around here lately, if you know what I mean, *Stink*."

I wanted to say, *For the last time, I don't smell!* But then I saw the dog grinning lopsidedly at me, and I shot him a devilish look.

"That's *Mr.* Stink," I said.

I waited until the bus pulled away, then strolled back home and up to my boy's bedroom. I had grown accustomed to taking a brief morning nap on his quilt.

That was when I saw it. I hissed.

Aaron's dark blue pillow had a deep indentation in it. As if a cat had been sitting on it recently.

And the cat had left a calling card.

A single long white whisker.

Authors' Addendum

THIS IS the first of a number of reports James Edward Bristlefur prepared shortly before his disappearance. "Mr. Stink," as his closest friends knew him, had many adventures in America and across the globe, and we are only now beginning to translate the large stack of materials found in his safe house.

We have tried to assemble his notes as accurately as possible. Any errors or omissions in the file are certainly our fault and not his.

Respectfully submitted,
Holm & Hamel
Special to MI9

Attention All Agents:
Have you seen Mr. Stink in your neighborhood?
Please report all sightings to findstink@stinkfiles.com.

THE TAIL ENDS HERE FOR NOW!

TURN THE PAGE FOR

A SNEAK PREVIEW OF . . .

Dossier 002:

TO SCRATCH A THIEF

I WAS CREEPING through the ducts of the Palace Hotel. I squeezed around a particularly tight turn and realized with alarm that the ducts seemed to be getting narrower. It was dusty and dark, and the scent of the cat I had been following was growing very faint. I paused and listened to the metallic echoes of my quarry's pawsteps receding into the distance.

Then the sounds stopped.

I held my breath and crept forward, thankful as the way ahead grew brighter. A panel in the side of the duct sent horizontal slashes of light spilling across the way.

Then I saw him, crouched, as if he were lying in wait for me. But his back was turned: he was facing the wrong way! I couldn't believe my good fortune.

I crept closer in perfect silence, and then I pounced. I was in midair when his head snapped around, and our eyes locked.

"Happy landings," he said. And laughed.

My paw landed on his tail, but the rest of me kept going.

I was slipping into a hole. It was a trap!

The cat's mocking voice echoed from above. "And now . . . say good-bye, James."

I landed on a metal grate several feet below and looked up. Before I could gather my feet under me, I saw his paw reach out and flip a switch. The grate beneath me opened to reveal a deep shaft. And at the bottom: an immense whirring fan with deadly blades!

I flung all four legs out, but my claws scrabbled uselessly against the slick metal sides of the shaft.

In a few seconds, I would be shredded. Pureed, even. Ground pâté of cat.

My life flashed before my eyes. One down and eight to go.

To think this had all started with cat food.